THIS LITTLE TIGER BOOK BELONGS TO:

KYLE

For Mum
~*MC*

For Cassie
~*VC*

LITTLE TIGER PRESS
An imprint of Magi Publications
1 The Coda Centre, 189 Munster Road, London SW6 6AW
www.littletigerpress.com

First published in Great Britain 2002
This edition published in 2002

ISBN 1 85430 809 2

A CIP catalogue record for this book is available from the British Library

Printed in China

4 6 8 10 9 7 5

WHERE THERE'S A BEAR, THERE'S TROUBLE!

Michael Catchpool & Vanessa Cabban

LITTLE TIGER PRESS

London

One brown bear saw
one yellow bee.
And one yellow bee
saw one brown bear.

One brown bear thought,
"Where there's a bee there must be honey . . .
sticky honey, yummy honey, drippy honey,
runny honey. I'll follow this bee as quietly
as can be."

One yellow bee thought,
"Where there's a bear there must be trouble.
I'll buzz off home as quickly as can be."
So one yellow bee buzzed off over
the dry stone wall . . .

followed by one brown bear, as quietly as could be on his softest tippy-toes.

Buzz! Buzz! Growl! Growl! Shhh!

Two greedy geese spotted one tiptoeing bear.
"Ha-ha," they thought. "Where there's a bear
there must be berries . . . ripe berries,
sweet berries, juicy berries, squishy berries.
Let's follow that bear as quietly as can be."

So two greedy geese followed one
brown bear, and one brown bear
followed one yellow bee,

Buzz! Buzz! Growl! Growl! Cackle! Cackle! Shhh!

all creeping along as quietly as can be.

Three shy mice spied two flapping geese.
"Ha-ha," they thought. "Where there
are geese there must be corn . . .

yellow corn, scrummy corn, crunchy
corn, tasty corn. Let's follow those geese
as quietly as can be."

Buzz! Buzz! Growl! Growl! Cackle! Cackle! Squeak.

So one yellow bee buzzed over the bramble bush, and one brown bear followed one yellow bee, and two greedy geese followed one brown bear, and three shy mice followed two greedy geese, all creeping along as quietly as could be!

Then one yellow bee buzzed
right into its nest . . .

*queak! Sh*hh'

and a thousand yellow
bees buzzed out!

One brown bear saw a thousand
yellow bees, and a thousand yellow
bees saw one brown bear.

One brown bear thought, "Where there's a swarm there must be

TROUBLE!

I'll run back home as quickly as can be."

"Help!" squawked the greedy geese.
"The bear is after us!"
And off they flapped,
back across the field.

"Help!" squeaked the shy mice.
"The geese are after us!"
And off they scrabbled
as quickly as could be.
But then . . .

Growl! Ouch!

Squawk! Hiss!

Squeak! Eek!

CRASH!

One brown bear fell over two greedy geese, and
two greedy geese fell over three shy mice.

And one yellow bee thought,
"I knew there'd be trouble!"

More fantastic books from Little Tiger Press

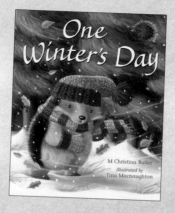

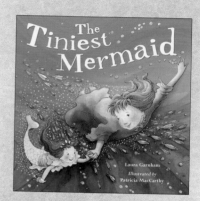

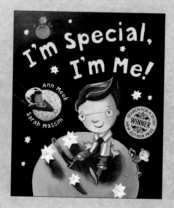

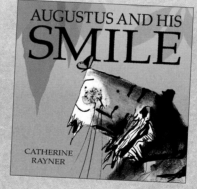

For information regarding the above titles or for our catalogue,
please contact us: Little Tiger Press, 1 The Coda Centre,
189 Munster Road, London SW6 6AW
Telephone: 020 7385 6333 • Fax: 020 7385 7333
E-mail: info@littletiger.co.uk • www.littletigerpress.com